Meet . . .

Mum

Dad

Granny

Granny's husband, Lancelot

And, of course, me

We were all eating our lunch when . . .

Jeremy Strong once worked in a bakery, putting the jam into three thousand doughnuts every night. Now he puts the jam in stories instead, which he finds much more exciting. At the age of three, he fell out of a first-floor bedroom window and landed on his head. His mother says that this damaged him for the rest of his life and refuses to take any responsibility. He loves writing stories because he says it is 'the only time you alone have complete control and can make anything happen'. His ambition is to make you laugh (or at least snuffle). Jeremy Strong lives in Kent with his wife, Susan, a cat or two, and something in the attic that makes scratching noises at night, but he hasn't found out what it is yet.

Some other books by Jeremy Strong

DINOSAUR POX

THE HUNDRED-MILE-AN-HOUR DOG

MY DAD'S GOT AN ALLIGATOR!

MY GRANNY'S GREAT ESCAPE

I'M TELLING YOU THEY'RE ALIENS!

THERE'S A PHARAOH IN OUR BATH!

THERE'S A VIKING IN MY BED

Jeremy Strong

My Mum's Going to Explode!

PUFFIN BOOKS

*With many thanks to my mother for the story
about the sausages. it really happened.
This story is for all Puffin poppers,
especially Helen D. and Charlotte B.*

PUFFIN BOOKS

Published by the Penguin Group
Penguin Books Ltd, 80 Strand, London WC2R 0RL, England
Penguin Putnam Inc., 375 Hudson Street, New York, New York 10014, USA
Penguin Books Australia Ltd, 250 Camberwell Road, Camberwell, Victoria 3124, Australia
Penguin Books Canada Ltd, 10 Alcorn Avenue, Toronto, Ontario, Canada M4V 3B2
Penguin Books India (P) Ltd, 11 Community Centre, Panchsheel Park, New Delhi – 110 017, India
Penguin Books (NZ) Ltd, Cnr Rosedale and Airborne Roads, Albany, Auckland, New Zealand
Penguin Books (South Africa) (Pty) Ltd, 24 Sturdee Avenue, Rosebank 2196, South Africa

Penguin Books Ltd, Registered Offices: 80 Strand, London WC2R 0RL, England

www.penguin.com

First published by A & C Black 1999
Published in Puffin Books 2001

14

Text copyright © Jeremy Strong, 2001
Illustrations copyright © Rowan Clifford, 2001
Illustrations based on the original artwork of Nick Sharratt © Nick Sharratt, 2001
All rights reserved

The moral right of the author has been asserted

Set in 14/23 Baskerville

Made and printed in England by Clays Ltd, St Ives plc

British Library Cataloguing in Publication Data
A CIP catalogue record for this book is available from the British Library

ISBN 0–141–31053–7

Contents

1 August: Mum Makes an Announcement

Big news from my family! There's no easy way to tell you, so sit down and brace yourself. My mum's …

… Well, I guess that first of all I'd better tell you how we found out.

There we were – me, Mum and Dad, just about to sit down and eat our lunch with Granny and Lancelot. They're living with us at the moment because they had a small problem with their house. Well, actually, it wasn't really a *small* problem but a pretty big one – their house fell down. A whopping great hole opened up in their garden and half their house fell into it. So, they've moved in with us until they find a new house.

It's nice having them back. Granny

always makes me laugh, and Lancelot is a brilliant cook. He might be a sixty-five-year-old Hell's Angel, but I have to admit that  he's a whizz at the stove. He wears a special Hell's Angel apron when he's in the kitchen. It's got silver studs that say:

BURN, BABY, BURN

Lancelot had just dished up some chicken in white-wine sauce when Mum made the announcement.

'I'm pregnant,' she said, as if it was something that happened every day, and carried on eating.

Dad was so surprised he dropped his cutlery. The knife landed on a particularly sloppy bit of the plate and splattered white-wine sauce all over Mum. A split second later, Dad's fork landed handle first and broke the plate. The rest of the sauce spilled on to the table, spread to the edge and dribbled into his lap.

My dad's like that. Things happen to him that don't happen to anyone else. He's great!

Granny wagged a finger at him. 'Don't play with your food, Ronald! I thought a big boy like you would be more sensible.' She turned to my mum. 'What was that you said, dear?'

'I'm going to have a baby.'

Granny's eyes popped. 'You've got

rabies? Oh dear.' She reached across the
table and patted Mum's arm. 'Never mind,
I've got some nice handcream upstairs.'

RABIES?

Mum gave me a long-suffering look.
Granny's a bit deaf and sometimes she gets
rather muddled. Mind you, I don't know
what good handcream is if you've got
rabies.

'Look at the mess you've
made, Ronald,' Granny went
on, as if my dad were still a
little boy. 'I think you should
take Brenda to the doctor. She's got
rabies. I have some cream she can use, but it
will only treat the spots. I haven't got
anything for foaming at the mouth.'

Luckily, at this point, Lancelot took over. He's been married to Granny for a year now and he knows what she's like. He put his mouth to her left ear and bellowed, 'Brenda's pregnant! She's going to have a baby!'

Granny jumped back in her chair. 'There's no need to shout. I'm not deaf.'

By this time Dad seemed to have slipped into a state of deep shock. He just sat there, rocking slightly from side to side. His eyes had gone glassy. Mum flicked her fingers in front of his face. 'Hello? Hello? Is anyone in?'

Dad slowly turned and gazed at her. 'A baby?' he croaked. 'How did that happen?'

I giggled, and Mum's eyebrows slid up her head. 'I don't think I'll go into any details at the lunch table, but you were involved, Ron.'

Lancelot gave my dad a nudge. 'Well done! Another nipper in the family!'

I didn't like the way this was going. Another nipper? *I'm* not a nipper! Is that what they think? I'm ten!

Granny began clapping her hands with delight and bouncing up and down on her chair. 'Oooh! I'm going to be a granny!' she cried.

'You already are a granny, Granny,' I pointed out.

She stopped for a moment. 'Oh yes. So I am! But it's very exciting, isn't it?'

I gave her a weak smile, but inside I was thinking that it wasn't very exciting at all. Worrying? Yes. Depressing? Yes. Exciting? I don't think so. I glanced round the table. Everyone was smiling. Everyone seemed over the moon.

All except for me and Dad. Dad gazed down into his lap.

'I think I've wet myself,' he said glumly.

2 Big Changes

You should have heard Granny today. She really got Dad wound up. She's been having a great time. The new baby is going to mean big changes around here. For a start, Granny and Lancelot will have to hurry up and find a place of their own. Their house may have fallen down, but the baby is going into the spare room, and that's where Granny and Lancelot are.

Granny made such a fuss! She doesn't mind at all really. I think she just wanted to have a bit of fun. She stood in the middle of the front room, with her head down, looking lost, lonely and miserable.

'We're being thrown out,' she wailed.

'It's not like that,' said Dad. 'You know it isn't.'

'Thrown out into the cold.'

Dad glared at her. 'It's August, Mother. It's mid-summer and it's not cold.'

'Thrown out without food or shelter.' Granny winked at me and began sniffing.

'*Sniff!* I suppose we could build ourselves a little shelter in the far corner of the back garden. *Sniff! Sniff!* We could use a few sticks, and make a roof with grass and old leaves. *Sniff!* But I'm sure the rain will come in.' Granny plucked at Dad's sleeve

pathetically. 'We'd have to go behind the bushes for a wee. Would you mind very much?'

'I'm not having you living in the corner of the garden like a pair of trolls!' cried Dad.

'Oh dear. *Sniff!* Well, I suppose we *could* get a little caravan or something. We could put it on the lawn in front of the house. Then we could come in here for baths and meals and you could do our washing for us and ...'

'You're not living in a caravan in the front garden either!' yelled Dad. 'Don't be so ridiculous.'

I could see that Granny was about to start laughing. 'You're awfully upset, aren't you, Ron? I was only pulling your leg, you know.' Dad sat hunched in the armchair, seething quietly. 'Are you upset about the new baby?'

'Yes. No! I don't know. It takes a bit of getting used to.'

I knew just how he felt. He was right. It did take a lot of getting used to. I'd been the only child in the house since I was born. It was always Mum, Dad and me. (I'm not counting Granny and Lancelot. They're sort of extras.) Now it was going to be Mum, Dad, me and – IT.

We didn't even know if it was going to be a boy or a girl.

'I don't want to know,' said Mum. 'I want it to be a surprise.'

'It already is a surprise,' snapped Dad, without thinking.

Mum watched him nervously. 'You do want this baby, don't you, Ronald?'

Dad took a deep breath and nodded. 'Yes, of course I do.' He went across to Mum and gave her a big hug. It looked like they were getting soppy so I left.

I went to see if I could find Lancelot. He was out in the garage, tinkering with his motorbike. It's an ancient beast of a thing. It's called a Matchless, and it's got a sidecar that Granny sits in when they go out. They've both got leather jackets and everything. Lancelot's has got fringed sleeves and studs.

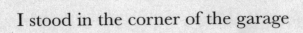

I stood in the corner of the garage

while Lancelot grunted at his bike. He was too busy talking to it to take much notice of me. He always talks to his bike.

'So, what's up with you then, my pretty? Got a bit wet round your plugs? I'll get you sorted out, don't you worry.'

Lancelot noticed me hanging about. 'Here you are,' he said, handing over a spark plug. 'See if you can clean up those ends so that they're nice and shiny. Can't get a spark out of a dirty plug.' He bent back over the bike while I rubbed away.

'So,' he said, as if he was still talking to the bike. 'There's going to be a new baby in the family. How do you feel about that?'

'Don't know.'

'Hmmm. Bit of a puzzler, eh?'

'Is that all right?' I showed him the plug.

'That's lovely. There's another one on the bench that needs doing. What would you prefer, a brother or a sister?'

I was silent. I wanted to say 'neither'.

Lancelot peered up at me. He must have seen the look on my face, and it made him chuckle. 'You'd rather there was no baby at all! Don't worry, there's nothing wrong in feeling like that.'

'But I don't want to,' I said, and I didn't.

'It takes a bit of getting used to,' said Lancelot. 'Look at your dad. It threw him when he found out, and he's grown-up.'

'Granny's been teasing him. She said Dad was throwing you two out of the house. She told him she was going to build a shelter out of twigs in the back garden.'

Lancelot burst out laughing. 'That's my babe! She's a cracker, your gran! And I'll tell you something else about her. She's not as deaf as she pretends to be!'

'We all know that,' I said, handing over the second plug. Lancelot screwed it into place. He heaved himself on to the seat and gave the bike a hefty kick-start.

You should have heard the noise! It was wonderful; a fabulous, roaring animal, throbbing away in the garage, desperate for freedom. Lancelot tossed me a crash helmet.

'Let's hit the road. I've got some serious house hunting to do. I don't want to end up living in a twig hut!'

3 September: Introducing Imelda

Mum's gone all weird on us. She's been reading billions of books about baby care. She says the baby can hear things even while it's inside her. She's been singing to it, and now she wants to read stories to it. Mad or what?!

'You can read the baby a story, Nicholas, if you like.'

'It's OK, Mum.'

'The baby would like you to read it a story.' Mum's voice took on a hard edge.

'Mum, how do you know?'

Her face began to darken. 'I just *know*,' she said.

'Anyway, it says so in one of my books. If you read to it before it's born it will help make it more intelligent.' Her eyes fixed on mine. 'Are you going to read it a story or not?'

'I've got homework to do,' I lied, and went upstairs. I could hear Mum in the front room talking to her tummy. I shut my bedroom door. What kind of madhouse am I in? You see, it's not just the reading stories to a stomach. There are other things too.

Mum's unearthed this big doll she had when she was a child. You should see it. It's enough to give you nightmares! One eye is permanently half shut. Mum says it's been like that ever since she was a little girl.

'Some strawberry jam got stuck behind her eye,' she explained, as if it were quite normal.

The doll's half bald as well. I suppose she once had a mass of carroty coloured curls, but now she has just a few straggly bits and lots of holes in her head where the hair has fallen out. She's got a horrible red mouth. It's tiny and all puckered up, as if it's about to kiss you. Urgh!

And then there's the missing leg. Don't ask me where it's gone.

So, as you can see, the doll is not exactly appealing. She used to have an ancient dress that stuck out from her waist a bit like a ballet frock, until it fell off. So now she doesn't wear anything. I am surprised she hasn't been arrested going around like that!

The doll's called Imelda, and Mum has told Dad and me to look after her. Can you imagine!

Mum wants us to pretend that Imelda is the real thing.

Dad dangled the doll by her single leg. 'We can't look after this!'

'Don't hold her like that,' shouted Mum. 'She's upside down. You'll hurt her. Look, she's crying now.' Mum snatched Imelda from Dad and held her in her arms. 'There, there. Is he a big nasty gorilla? Yes, he is, isn't he!'

Mum frowned across at Dad. 'She says
you're a big nasty gorilla.'

'Brenda, she's a doll. She's a bald, ugly
doll with one leg, and she can't speak.'

Mum fixed Dad with a long stare. 'I
know she's a doll, Ron, but we are going to
pretend that she is a real baby. You and
Nicholas will look after Imelda.'

'But why, Mum?' I whined.

'It will be a good way for you both to
get used to having a new baby in the house.
It says so in one of my books. I want you to
feed Imelda, to bath her
and to change her
nappies.'

Dad collapsed with hysterics. 'You're mad!' he cried. 'If we give her a bath the rest of her hair will probably fall out. And how can we put a nappy on a doll with one leg? It will fall down!'

By this time I was in hysterics too, but Mum was not amused. She simply held out Imelda for me to take.

'And don't forget to burp her,' said Mum, as she swept from the room.

Dad and I looked at each other and burst out laughing again, but it still left me holding the baby.

'What are we going to do, Dad?'

'We will do as your mother asks, Nicholas, because if we don't, life in this house will get even worse than it is already.' Dad thought for a few moments. 'I'll tell you what though. It could be fun.'

'Yeah?' Fun? Looking after an ancient doll?

'We could have races, you and me.'

'What sort of races?' I asked.

'Nappy-changing races. We could see who's the fastest.'

I looked at Dad. Nappy-changing races. What would he think of next? 'You can have first go,' I muttered.

So, things are a bit strange at the moment.

I've got Imelda tucked up in a little cot in the corner of my room. She sleeps with one eye half open, which makes me feel uncomfortable. It's as if she's watching me all the time. I'm sure she knows I hate her.

4 All About Frog
Shortening

Good news! Lancelot and Granny have
found a house. We all went to see it today.
Even Mr and Mrs Tugg came along. I
haven't mentioned them yet, have I? They're
our next-door neighbours. We used to be at
war with them, because Mr Tugg was always
complaining about my dad.

However, ever since Granny and
Lancelot got married, things have been a
little more friendly. The thing is, Lancelot is
Mr Tugg's father. You'd never guess it, not in
a million years. I mean, Mr Tugg is, I don't
know, Mr Normal, I suppose. He always
does everything in just the right way. His
garden is so neat and perfect it looks like
something cut out of a magazine.

You'd never think that he and Lancelot

were father and son. I told you Lancelot's a
Hell's Angel. He's got his hair in a ponytail,
and a large carrot tattooed on his left
shoulder blade. I know that sounds a bit
odd, but Lancelot used to be in the navy. He
was sent to Hong Kong, and while he was
out there he had this tattoo
done.

'I asked for a
parrot,' he told me, 'but
I don't think the tattoo
man heard me
properly.'

Anyhow, we went to
see the house they were going to
buy. We all met up outside, and the first
thing that Mr Tugg noticed was
that Lancelot had a ring in
one ear. He must have had his
ear pierced earlier that
afternoon.

Mr Tugg shuddered. 'Father, I do wish you would be a bit more …'

'Boring?' suggested Lancelot.

'No! I was going to say respectable. Goodness knows what these people here will make of you.' Mr Tugg shook his head in despair.

'It's rather pretty,' said Mrs Tugg.

'No, it isn't. It's ridiculous!' her husband shouted.

My dad was delighted to see how upset Mr Tugg was becoming, and he gave Gran a smug smile. 'At least you haven't got one,' he observed.

Granny pulled up the bottom of her jumper and tugged at her vest. 'There. What do you think of that?' Granny had a ring through her belly button!

Mum screamed and clutched her own tummy. 'Oh, how could you!'

'That's really cool, Gran!' I said.

'It's not cool at all!' everyone else shouted. (I mean my parents and the Tugg Team.)

At that moment, the front door opened and the owners of the house peered out at us, wondering what on earth we were up to. Granny still had her jumper pulled halfway up her chest. Dad hastily leaped in front of her and beamed at the house owners.

'Hello!' he cried. 'We've come to look at your house.'

'Right. Good afternoon. I'm Bernard Throgmorton and this is my wife, Thelma.'

Mrs Throgmorton's head dipped and rose, dipped and rose as she nodded. She reminded me of a stork, a very polite stork. She was tall and thin, with a sharp nose.

Mr Throgmorton stood in the doorway surveying us. He didn't seem to like the look of the two Hell's Angels. 'Are they with you?' he asked Mr Tugg, and the poor man gave an embarrassed nod.

'They'd better wait outside,' snapped Mr Throgmorton. 'They look smelly.'

Dad put on his most polite smile. 'Actually, *they* are the

house buyers. This is my mother, and this is
her husband. Lancelot is the father of Mr
Tugg here.'

'That's not possible,' snapped Bernard
Throgmorton. 'I mean, they're – they look
awful.'

Lancelot strode to the front and
whipped off his shades. He eyeballed Mr
Throgmorton. 'I've got a scar,' he growled.
'Got it in a knife fight. The other geezer's
dead. Lots of blood. Can we come in?
Thank you!'

Bernard staggered back as Lancelot
and Granny made their way into the hall.
Dad followed.

Bernard Throgmorton had gone white. 'Did he really k, k, ki …?' he squeaked, and Dad nodded.

Of course Lancelot doesn't have a scar, and he wouldn't hurt a tadpole! But it shook Bernard Frogshortener. (That's what my dad called him after we got home!)

The house looked like it would be just the job. It had only two bedrooms, but it had a nice bit of garden and it was near us.

Granny and Lancelot loved it. So now they're sorted out. I'm glad they've got somewhere to live and it's not far away. I shall miss them when they go.

Mind you, I've always got Imelda for company. Not to mention the baby when it arrives. Lucky me.

5 November: Big Trouble

Boy, you should have heard the row today! I thought the house would fall down round our ears. We've all been in BIG TROUBLE WITH MUM.

The thing is, Mum's cooking has been all wonky for weeks now. She keeps giving us sausages to eat. She seems to have developed a craving for them. We're given sausages for breakfast, sausages for lunch and sausages for supper. It's driving us mad. Dad even pleaded with her, on his knees.

'Please, please, can we have something else to eat?'

'Sausages are very nice and I like them.'

Granny says that when women are expecting a baby they sometimes go through a phase like this. 'When I was expecting Ronald, I spent a whole month eating nothing but soap and sardines.'

'That's revolting, Granny!'

'Oh, I know, but I enjoyed it at the time. Don't worry about the sausages. Your mother will get over it eventually.'

It's all very well for Granny to say that, but those sausages were getting on our nerves. Mum wouldn't let Lancelot do any cooking either, because she knew he wouldn't do sausages.

I couldn't go on like that, so I started

hiding my sausages. I'd get them to the edge of the plate and then, when nobody was looking, I'd shove them up my sleeves. I'd get rid of them later. Sometimes I put them down the toilet and flushed them. I buried some in the garden, and the others I stuffed into litter bins on my way to school.

It was all going very well, but then Mum found out. It wasn't my fault. It was Dad's. He was so fed up he was doing the same thing. When nobody was looking at *him* he was sticking sausages inside the front of his shirt. If he had got rid of them like I did I don't think Mum would ever have found out. But Dad was so stupid. You know where he hid them?

In his chest of drawers, under his socks.

You can imagine what it was like after a month or so. The sausages were going all mouldy and beginning to stink. Mum kept saying she thought there was an odd smell in the bedroom. Dad said it was that time of year.

'What time of year?' asked Mum.

'The time of year for bad smells,' Dad said mysteriously.

Anyhow, Mum just happened to open Dad's drawer and discovered half a ton of mouldering sausages piled up in there. Talk about high drama! She went off like some mad tank, firing in all directions at once. She was furious.

'I wondered why you kept getting grease stains on the front of your shirt. You are a disgusting, disgusting man! How do you expect me to bring a new little baby into the house of a secret sausage-stasher?'

Dad was literally backed into a corner by all this, but Granny came to his rescue, much to my surprise.

'To tell you the truth, dear,' Granny began, 'Lancelot and I have rather gone off sausages ourselves.'

'Oh yes?' Mum looked daggers at her.

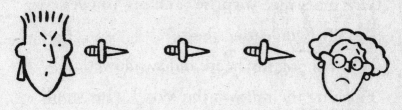

'Yes, dear. You see, it's not just Ronald. I can't let him get into trouble when we've been doing the same.'

Mum's jaw dropped. 'You're not telling me that you've been filling your drawers with sausages as well?'

'Not at all, dear, no. I've been putting them in my handbag.'

'Your handbag!'

'Yes. And then Lancelot has taken them away on his motorbike, down to the dump, for recycling.'

For a few seconds Mum was speechless. She gazed at Dad and Granny. Finally she turned to me. 'What have you been doing with your sausages, Nicholas? Give me a nice surprise. Tell me you've actually been eating them.'

I shook my head and swallowed. 'Flushing them down the loo,' I whispered. 'And burying them in the garden.' Mum glared at me as if I were a little boy.

'How old are you?'

'Ten.'

'Forty-five,' muttered Dad.

'And I'm sixty-three, dear,' added Granny, very matter-of-factly. 'I'm sorry, Brenda, but we are fed up with sausages.'

10   45   63

At least Granny was brave enough to speak out. That was when Mum realized that she had a problem, and the problem was *her*, not us. She was outnumbered for a start, and we all felt the same way. She sat down heavily in an armchair. Dad made a move towards her, but Mum waved him away.

'Leave me alone,' she growled. 'All of you. I don't even want to see you.'

We crept out of the room and Dad quietly shut the door. 'She'll get over it,' he said. 'Pregnancy makes women ever so moody, you know.'

Granny was halfway up the stairs, but now she stopped and leaned over the banisters. 'It's very easy for a man to say something like that, Ronald. You try carrying another human around inside yourself and see how it makes you feel.'

'Ouch,' muttered Dad.

So, we're all in the doghouse, but at least Mum is speaking to us again. She's agreed to let Lancelot do the cooking for the rest of us.

'And I'll cook my own sausages,' she huffed.

6 Dad Plays Up

I'm top of my class! I came first! To tell you the truth, there were only two of us being tested, but I still came top. Mum gave Dad and me a Baby-care Test. We took turns with Imelda and we had to:

1 *Change her nappy.*
2 *Bath her.*
3 *Change her clothes.*
4 *Strap her in a car safety seat.*
5 *Burp her.*

I wish you could have seen it. Mum had prepared a little surprise for us. Dad had to go first with the nappy changing. He was singing away and saying how easy it was. Then he unfastened the nappy and got the shock of his life.

'I put some mushy peas in there,' said Mum, as if it were the sort of thing she did every day. 'I thought it would make it more realistic.'

'It's revolting!' cried Dad.

'At least it doesn't smell, Ron. Surely you don't expect to be changing unsoiled nappies? Now, make sure you wipe Imelda clean before you put a fresh one on her.'

'But the peas have gone inside the hole where her leg was,' Dad whined.

'Clean her!'

'The nappy keeps slipping down. I told you it would. You need *two* legs to keep a nappy up.'

'You haven't fastened it properly,' Mum said. 'That's all.'

Dad went storming off and returned a few moments later with a roll of sellotape. He wound it round and round the nappy, across Imelda's chest and finally up and over both her shoulders. He picked up the doll and thrust her towards Mum.

'There,' he grunted. Mum took Imelda and examined her.

'One out of ten,' she said. 'Now it's Nicholas's turn.'

It was a bit messy, but I managed a better job than Dad, and Mum gave me eight, so I was pretty pleased. We did the bathing next, and that was all right, except that Dad played submarines with the doll, and I mean Imelda *was* the submarine.

43

'You've scored nought,' Mum told him. 'Nicholas, you did an excellent job. Ten out of ten.'

'That's not fair!' protested Dad.

'Ron, she is not a U-boat. She is a small, defenceless baby.'

'But the water went up her leg-hole and she sank!' protested Dad.

I think that after the bathing Dad decided he couldn't possibly win, so he just played up all the time. It was like having a really naughty kid there. He put Imelda's Babygro on her upside down. He strapped her in the car seat the wrong way round, so that she was facing the wrong way. And

when he came to burp her,
Dad thumped her so hard
the doll's head fell off.

OOPS!

I thought it was
really funny, but Mum
had that steely glint in
her eye. She sent me off to
play while she kept Dad
behind so that she could 'have words' with
him. I heard her telling him that he was a
show-off, a 'bad example', and that he
'should know better'. She made Dad stay in
and do it all again, properly.

She can be just like some of my
teachers.

The thing is though, Mum wants us to
pretend that Imelda is real, and we can't,
because she isn't! She's impossible to like. I
mean, she's half bald, she's got a leg missing,
and then there's that awful squiffy eye.

It will be different when the real baby

comes. I know it will. Listen, yesterday
evening Mum was watching telly when she
called me over. She took my hand, put it on
her stomach and held it there.

'What?' I said.

'Wait a moment. There!'

I felt a tiny nudge against my hand,
and then again. 'What is it?' I asked.

'The baby,' said Mum. 'Your brother
or sister. It's kicking.'

I kept my hand there a bit longer, feeling those little nudges, like someone tapping out a message. It was trying to talk to me. It was saying 'hello'!

That's how I know it will be OK when the baby comes.

7 December: Surprise, Surprise!

Oh boy! You will never, ever guess in a million years what happened today. It was as if Christmas arrived early.

Mum had to go into hospital for a check-up, and Dad and I went with her. I saw something truly astonishing. But I'd better start from the beginning.

My mum's getting quite big now. I mean, you can tell she's having a baby. Her tummy's swelling and she has to do things like bending down carefully. I asked her what it was like and she told me to imagine that I'd swallowed a carrier bag full of

shopping. It doesn't sound very comfortable, does it?

Anyhow, we all went trooping off to the hospital. I had to wait outside of course, in case I heard something I wasn't supposed to, ha ha. I could hear the nurse droning on for hours, asking Mum loads of questions. Finally the nurse gave Mum a scan, and I was allowed to come and look too.

Mum lay on a bed and the nurse rubbed some special jelly all over her swollen stomach. It was really gloopy-doopy! Then she got a scanner – it was a bit like one of those hand scanners you see in check-outs at shops. It made me laugh.

'They're going to price up your shopping bag, Mum.' She burst out laughing, but Dad and the nurse just gave us strange, blank looks.

'You're getting to be as daft as your father,' said Mum.

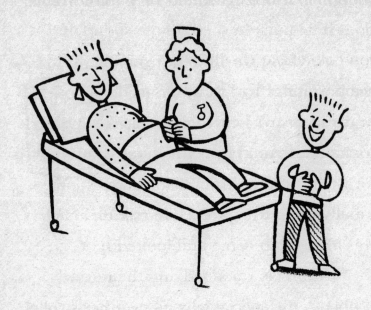

The nurse plopped this thing on to
Mum's belly and began moving it slowly.
There was a little TV monitor and this
flickering grey image came up on the screen.

At first it was like watching telly when
the aerial's not working. There was just
flickering grey fuzz everywhere. And then,
all of a sudden, there it was, a little baby!

IT WAS MOVING!

IT WAS KICKING ITS LEGS!

IT WAS SUCKING ITS THUMB!

The nurse turned up the sound and you could hear the baby's heart beating. You could hear my mum's heart too – great big booming  thing – and then there were these dainty little thuds going on. You could even see its ears and fingers and toes.

Mum was crying, but she had this huge smile on her face. Dad was squeezing her hand. He looked pretty choked too. As for me, I was just amazed. Something burst inside me, like one of those really, *really*, REALLY expensive fireworks, with hundreds of coloured star bursts and cascading showers of golden glitter. It exploded inside and rushed to every little corner of my body, right up to the very tips

51

of the hair on my head and down into my
toes. Even my toenails tingled!

Dad was staring at the monitor and
suddenly he gave a horrified croak. He
slowly lifted one arm and pointed at the
screen, with his finger
shaking uncontrollably.

'It … it … it's got
three arms!' he gasped.
'And two heads!'

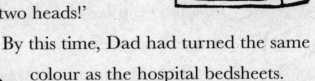

By this time, Dad had turned the same
colour as the hospital bedsheets.

His eyes flickered, rolled upwards
and he crumpled in a
heap on the floor.

The nurse
comforted Mum. 'It's all
right, he's just a bit shocked.'

'But the baby!' cried Mum.
'Look!' Sure enough, the baby was now
waving three arms at us.

'It looks like you're going to have twins,' said the nurse.

'Twins?' squeaked Mum, before going all limp. It was a good thing she was already lying down. The nurse pressed the red 'HELP' button and turned to me.

'Are you going to faint too?'

I shook my head. 'We weren't expecting twins,' I pointed out. 'It's a bit of a shock.'

'So it seems. Can you just hold your father's head for a moment, while I sort out your mother?' The nurse bustled around Mum while I sat on the floor holding Dad's head so that he was comfortable.

It's a strange world!

Luckily, another nurse arrived and took over from me. Dad soon came round and he was helped on to the trolley bed next to Mum. They made a right pair! I had the job of explaining to Dad that Mum was going to have twins.

'The second baby was hidden behind the first,' I told him. 'The nurse said that it happens like that quite often with twins.'

'I'd only just got used to the idea of one baby, let alone two,' he murmured. He

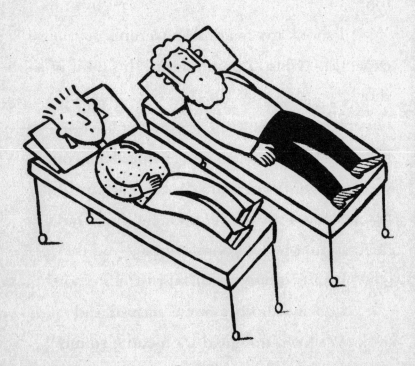

gave Mum a weak smile. 'Twins, eh? Who's a clever girl! Two presents for the price of one. Christmas has come early this year!'

Ever since we got home, Dad's been telling everyone. Granny was rather taken aback.

'Brenda's had a scan and you've seen tins? Are you sure, Ron? I don't know about these scan things, they didn't have them in my day, but I don't think they show you tins. Were they tins of baby food? I suppose that might make sense.'

'TWINS!' roared Lancelot, laughing like billy-o.

'Oh,' said Granny, and her face lit up. She patted Mum's hand. 'I am glad they're not tins, Brenda.'

My mum looked at Granny and they fell about laughing, and that started me off. We were back to the bags of shopping.

'Can you imagine it?' Mum giggled. 'I

might have had tins! "Is it a boy or a girl, nurse?" … "Actually, madam, it's pineapple chunks!"'

TINS?

It's been a totally brilliant day. Dad is really chuffed, and so am I. Mum's going to have twins and we still don't know whether they will be boys or girls. I've given Imelda back to Mum and told her I want the real

TWINS!

thing. I wish I could tell you how I feel, but it's weird. It's like my emotions are whizzing round and round, too fast to catch, too fast to hold, too fast to even know what they are. I can only think of one word to describe it, but it seems much, much too small to tell you how I really feel.

HAPPY

Happy.

8 February: Dad Has a Baby

You should see my mum now! I think she's going to explode. She's the size of an elephant. She goes waddling round very slowly, holding her belly. You can see her coming almost a week before she arrives! You get this glimpse of a giant whale entering the room, and the rest of Mum follows, days later.

Dad's been making fun of her, but Mum got her own back this afternoon, with Granny's help.

'It's no joke carrying two babies around,' she complained. 'I wish you were me.'

I think Granny must have heard her
because she went wandering off for a while.
When she came back she was holding a
balloon. It was a green one, left over from
Christmas, and it hadn't been blown up yet.

'I think this might help,' Granny said.
'Ronald, you come with me for a moment.'

'This all looks very mysterious,' Dad
murmured suspiciously. 'What are you going
to do?'

'She's up to something,' agreed
Lancelot, giving me a wink. 'That's my
babe!'

'Just follow me,'
said Granny, and the two
of them disappeared
through to the
kitchen.

I could
hear them talking
to each other out there.

OH RONALD?

Dad's voice was getting louder. He was
obviously upset. Granny's voice was quieter,
but insistent. Finally, Granny came back and
settled down in her armchair, but where was
Dad? What was he up to? We watched and
waited.

Finally the door slowly swung open.
And then Dad appeared,
stomach first. His belly was as
big and swollen as Mum's. He
waddled towards a chair.

'Ron! What
have you done?'
giggled Mum.

Dad
looked daggers at
Granny. 'It's my
mother's idea,' he
hissed, holding his huge
belly. 'I've got a balloon
stuck up my jumper,

filled with water. It's supposed to be like carrying twins, but it makes me feel stupid and uncomfortable.'

'In that case you know just how I feel,' said Mum. 'What a clever idea, Gran. Well done.'

You can imagine what it was like after that. Mum asked Dad when the baby was due. I wanted to know if it was going to be a boy balloon or a girl. Lancelot asked Dad what he was going to call it when it was born.

'Pop! That would be a good name for a balloon,' said Lancelot. 'Or how about Huffenpuff?'

Dad scowled at everyone and eased himself into a chair. 'Do I have to keep this thing stuck up here?'

'Yes, dear. Poor Brenda has had to do it for months now.' Granny threw me a glance. 'And if you think it's funny, Nicholas, there is another balloon here.' That wiped the grin off my face! No way was I going to be pregnant with a balloon.

We were just settling down to watch some telly when the front doorbell went. Dad struggled up.

It was Mr Tugg. He gawped at Dad, who was standing there holding his belly. Dad really enjoyed his surprise. He rubbed one hand gently across his stomach. 'I'm having twins,' he boasted to our neighbour. 'Pop and Huffenpuff.'

'Don't be silly. Men don't have babies.'
Mr Tugg eyed my father. 'Now then, I've
just had a telephone call, and you will never
guess who it was from.'

'Father Christmas?' suggested Dad.
'Don't tell me. He ate the mince pie you left
out for him and now he's got food
poisoning.'

Mr Tugg ignored him. 'It was that very
nice man with the house that my father and
your mother wish to buy, Mr Throgmorton.'

'Oh yes, Frogshortener,' said Dad,
nodding.

'Frogmortoner,' corrected Mr Tugg.
'Now you've got me doing it. The long and
short of it is …'

'… it must have been elastic,' Dad
butted in.

'What?' Mr Tugg looked perplexed.

'The frog,' said Dad.

'What frog?'

'The elastic one that was being made long and then short.'

'What are you talking about?' Mr Tugg shook his head violently, as if his ears had just been invaded by swarms of bees.

'Frogs,' said Dad. 'What are you talking about?'

FROGS

Mr Tugg's eyes narrowed dangerously. He always found it difficult to tell if my dad was winding him up or if he was simply

being stupid. But Dad looked so natural, apart from the balloon stuck up his jumper of course.

'I sometimes wonder what kind of mad world you live in,' Mr Tugg said. 'Please don't interrupt me this time. Mr Throgshortener, I mean Throgmorton, has phoned to say that he is refusing to sell them his house.'

Granny and Lancelot came hurrying

to the door. 'But it was just what we wanted,' said Lancelot. 'Why?'

Mr Tugg smiled grimly. 'He said that they lived in a nice neighbourhood and they didn't want it spoiled by having Hell's Angels living there.' He frowned at Gran. 'It's your mother's fault.'

Dad bristled. 'My mother? It's your father causing the trouble. He's the one with the motorbike, *and* the ponytail, *and* the earring, not to mention a carrot on his shoulder.'

'Maybe, but *your* mother's got a ring through her belly button! If you remember, she showed them on their doorstep!' Mr Tugg

angrily prodded Dad to make his point. There was a muffled **SPLOP!!** and the balloon burst. An entire lake sploshed out of Dad's jumper and slopped down his trousers *and* Mr Tugg's.

Dad shook his jumper and a shrivelled shred of green rubber fell into the puddle gathering round his feet. Dad stared down at it. 'That was my baby balloon,' he complained to our neighbour.

'Pop and Huffenpuff,' added Lancelot dolefully.

'You're not from this planet,' muttered Mr Tugg. He turned on his heels and squelched back to his house, desperately trying to appear dignified.

9 March: Dad Plays Up Again

Granny and Lancelot have moved out. It's really strange without them. Things have been so busy around here. It feels like we've done nothing but rush about ever since Christmas.

First of all, we had that unexpected news about the twins, so Mum and Dad had to get in extra supplies. They had to take the new pushchair back for a start, and swop it for a twin-buggy. We got another cot and more baby blankets and clothes. You should see inside the wardrobe in The Baby Zone. (That's what we've called the twins' bedroom.) Open the wardrobe door and ten tons of nappies fall on top of you!

Meanwhile, Granny and Lancelot have been whizzing about on the Matchless,

searching for another house. It was a real
shame about that horrible Mr Throgmorton.
I know Gran and Lancelot look a bit
different, but when you know them they are
such nice people. Neither of them would
hurt a fly. When I grow up I shall try not to
judge people by appearances. After all, look
at my dad. You'd think he was quite normal.
Some joke! You want to know what he's
been up to now? He's been thrown out of
Mum's exercise class.

There's this kind of baby club that
Mum and Dad have been going to each

week. It's for women who are expecting a baby, and their partners. They do floor exercises to strengthen tummy muscles – stuff like that. Mum practises them at home every day.

The classes are for the fathers as well. Dad says that they teach you how to help your partner when she goes into labour.

'What's labour?' I asked.

'That's when the baby gets born.'

'Why is it called labour?'

'Because it's hard work,' Mum butted in.

Anyhow, they were at this exercise class, and Dad was fooling about as usual. (This is what Mum told me afterwards.) Apparently, Dad had stuffed Imelda under his jumper and sneaked her in. (You remember Imelda? How could anyone forget!)

Halfway through the class, Dad started to pretend that he had gone into labour and

he was having a baby. He whipped out
Imelda and screeched at everyone. 'Oh no!
She's left a leg behind! It must be up here
somewhere! Quick, somebody help me!' He
began rummaging around up his jumper.

The midwife in charge of the class was
furious. She went steaming towards Dad,
shouting at him to stop. Most of the class

were in hysterics, and one lady found it so funny she went into labour on the spot! The midwife had to call an ambulance.

Dad's been banned from ever attending again. Mum wasn't very pleased with him, but I think she found it funny too. That's the thing with my mum. She can't help laughing at Dad's antics, even when he's being embarrassing. He certainly makes life interesting.

But I was going to tell you about
Granny and Lancelot's new house. Well, it's
not really a house at all. It's a house with a
shop. They've bought a motorbike business.

Lancelot saw an advertisement, quite
by chance. They had
just bought some
fish and chips, and
they were eating
them out of this old
newspaper, and there

was this advert; greasy, but still readable.

BUSINESS FOR SALE
Matchless Spares

Due to illness the owner is forced to sell
this successful business.

Vintage Matchless-motorbike spares sold and
delivered to the United Kingdom,
North America, Canada, Japan,
Australia and South Africa.
Small house included.

It's been like a dream come true for Lancelot, and Granny too. They love motorbikes and Lance knows almost everything there is to know about Matchless bikes. They're not made any more, and that means that spare parts are big business, right across the world.

I think it's great, and so does everyone else. Even Mr Tugg thinks it's a good idea, but that's only because he doesn't like having Hell's Angels living next to him.

The sale went through quickly and they've moved out. Ever since then we've been busy turning their old room into The Baby Zone. The only problem we had was what colour to paint it.

'Pink for a girl,' said Mum.

'Blue for a boy,' said Dad.

I reckon that's daft. I'm a boy, and I prefer yellow, but in the end the room was painted with blue and pink stripes. It looked

awful! Mum and Dad immediately started
again and painted it yellow all over, which is
what I suggested in the first place. It looks
much better.

All we need now is something to put
in it.

10 April: B-Day

Phew! What a day, or should I say night?
Things started happening towards the end of
the afternoon. Mum kept clutching her
stomach. She'd been doing this on and off
since morning, but now it was happening
every hour or so. She'd take quick deep
breaths and hold on to something, anything
– the doorpost, a cupboard, even me.

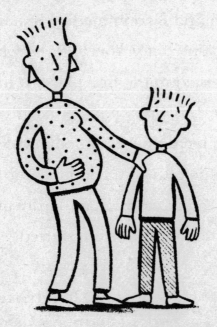

'What's up, Mum?'

'I'm going into labour, Nick. The twins are coming.'

I thought she meant straight away and got a bit worried, but Mum said it would be a while yet. 'Ask your father to cook tea, will you? I can't manage it tonight.'

My heart sank. Dad's not much of a cook, it has to be said. He stood in the kitchen and peered gloomily into the cupboards. Finally he shut the cupboard doors and picked up the telephone.

'Why don't we order some pizzas and have them delivered?'

As far as I was concerned anything was better than letting Dad cook. Mum seemed to think it was a good idea, so Dad ordered three pizzas. He had hardly put down the phone when Mum started moaning.

'Ohhhhhh! Ahhhhhh! Urrrrrrrrr!' She

was clutching her stomach and holding on to Dad. I could see the panic setting in on his face.

'What shall I do? What shall I do?'

Mum got her breath back. 'I think we'd better get to the hospital, Ron. I'm sure the twins are on the way. I've packed an overnight bag. It's on our bed upstairs.'

'I'll get it!' I shouted, and raced up.

Dad rang Granny and Lancelot to tell them what was happening. They were supposed to come over and look after me when Mum went into hospital, but there was no reply.

'They must be out,' Dad shouted, which was pretty obvious. 'You'll have to come with us, Nick. You can't stay here on your own.'

Dad helped Mum out to the car. She managed to ease herself into the front seat, but only after Dad had pushed it back as far as it would go. I leaped into the back. Dad started the car. It moved about one metre and then stopped. Dad tried to get it going, but all it would do was cough and splutter.

'Ooooh! Aaaah!' went Mum. 'Get me to the hospital, Ron!'

'The car won't go, the car won't go,' he yelled.

'Ron, I'm not in the mood for jokes. Please can you just take me to the hospital?'

'It's not a joke,' screamed Dad. 'It's an emergency!'

He opened the bonnet. He stared at the engine. He cursed the car. He kicked it, and still it wouldn't start.

'Ohhhhhh! Eeeeeeee!' went Mum, holding her huge belly in both hands.

'Dad, I'll ask the Tuggs! They've got a car!' I whizzed round next door and banged on the door. 'Open up! Please!'

But there was no answer. I banged and banged. I peered through the windows, but the house was in darkness and I couldn't see or hear anything. I raced back to the others.

'They must be out!' I cried.

'I'll call an ambulance,' said Dad, and he dashed back indoors.

'Eeeeeeee-ooooooooh!' went Mum, sounding rather like an ambulance herself. 'Hurry, hurry, please hurry!'

'It's all right, Mum, it will be all right.'

I know Mum was desperate to believe me, but she couldn't. She shook her head. 'Nothing is ever all right when your dad is around, Nicholas. Surely you know that by now?'

At that moment there was a *'beep'* from the road and the pizza delivery arrived. The pizza man had just got out when Dad came rushing back from the house. He seized the

pizza man by the shoulders and shoved him back into the van.

'You've got to help us,' said Dad, and he explained everything.

'I'm not allowed to carry passengers,' said the pizza man. Then he saw the look on Dad's face. It was a look that said: *If-you-don't-take-us-to-the-hospital-in-your-van-I-will-personally-kill-you-with-my-bare-hands-and-make-you-into-pizza-topping.*

Dad opened up the rear of the van and we helped Mum to climb in. She lay back on a pile of pizza cartons. I slipped into the

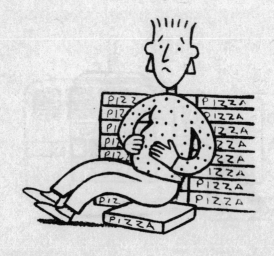

front and we set off. The drive to the
hospital seemed to take forever. I asked the
van man if he couldn't go any faster. He
shook his head.

'Pizza sauce curdles if it travels at more
than forty miles an hour,' he said. 'Not many
people know that.'

I spotted some flashing lights ahead
and they seemed to be coming towards us.
'It's the ambulance,' I cried. 'Quick, flash
them with your headlamps. Get them to
stop.'

We managed to stop the ambulance
and the pizza man was busily telling the

ambulance driver what was happening while
the paramedics took a look in the back of
the van.

'Urrrrrrrrrrrrrr! Arrrrrrrrrrrrr!' went
Mum.

'We can't move her,' they said. 'The
baby's due any second.' One of them turned
to Dad. 'We shall need your help. Grab this,
will you, and give me a hand up.'

The paramedic handed Dad some
bags of equipment and struggled into the
back with my parents. 'OK, son, you follow
us to the hospital in the ambulance.'

He pulled the door shut.

So they went off in the pizza van and I
had to follow behind, all by myself. (Apart
from the driver of course.) I sat there
thinking. It wouldn't be long now, and then I
wouldn't be the only child in my family any
more. I'd be a brother – a big brother. The
twins would be so much younger than me.

I'd have to look after them. Would I really change their nappies? Without wanting to throw up? The mushy peas were pretty bad, but what about when it was for real?

I suddenly realized I was sitting there and smiling, all to myself. I bet I could do a better job than Dad! I reckoned he'd run a mile rather than go near a nappy. He'd be brilliant at making the twins laugh, and telling them jokes and playing with them. But nappies were definitely not Dad's idea of a good time. So I'd have to do it. I'd look after them, whatever they were, my brothers or sisters. They would be my family.

My eyes were focused on the back of the pizza van, which was just ahead of us. I was wondering what was happening inside. Was Mum all right?

It seemed like hours before we reached the hospital. At last the van swept up to the main door, and screeched to a halt. Hospital

staff came rushing out. The doors of the
pizza van were flung open and Dad
appeared. He had such a soppy grin on his
face.

'I've got a delivery for you!' he
shouted at the medics. 'Three cheese and
tomato pizzas and two babies! I'm a father!'

I rushed to the van and peered in.
Mum was sitting up in the back, resting
against a pile of pizza boxes. She had a baby
in each arm, and she looked tired and
happy, like some kind of angel that had just

produced a miracle in the back of a pizza
van.

'You can come in,' she said, and I
crawled inside.

The babies were so dinky, like teeny
tiny pink people! It was hard to imagine that
they would grow as big as me, let alone even
bigger. Dad crawled in beside me and
slipped an arm round Mum.

'It's about time you two did something
useful,' said Mum. 'You can have one each
and give me a bit of a break. Put one hand

under her head, Nicholas. She needs to be supported. That's it.'

I gazed down at the pink bundle wriggling in my arms. I stroked her little hand with one finger. The baby grabbed it and held on tightly, as if she didn't want to lose me. 'Are they girls then?' I asked.

Mum leaned back against the pile of boxes and closed her eyes sleepily. 'Not at all. You've got a baby sister and a baby brother. One of each. How's that?'

'That's just about right.' I smiled. 'Brilliant.'

11 Happy Families

We're back home now, all five of us. Mum and Dad have been arguing over names.

'Brenda and Ronald,' said Dad.

'Don't be silly. They're our names.'

'I know,' said Dad. 'But what about Brenda and Ronald Junior.'

'Horrible. I like Clarissa and Justin.'

'Clarissa and Justin? Oooh, la-de-dah!'

Mum shot him a cross look. 'They are not la-de-dah, you silly man. They're nice names. I think "Clarissa" is very pretty. And Justin sounds like he's clever.'

Dad threw his arms up in despair. He knew that they would never agree.

However, they did. It took a week and a half, but eventually Mum and Dad decided what to call the twins: James and Rebecca. Nice, straightforward names. The only problem was that by this time Dad had given them both nicknames, and Dad's nicknames seem to have stuck.

You know what he calls them?

Cheese and Tomato.